Once Upon a Unicorn

By Madeline L. Stout

Book 1

Published by Fantasia Divinity © 2017

Printed in the United States of America

First Printing, 2017

ISBN-13: 978-1548772888

ISBN-10: 1548772887

Cover © Polyankakul 2017

Edited by Amber M. Simpson

Once Upon a Unicorn © Madeline L. Stout, 2017

Fantasia Divinity
www.fantasiadivinitymagazine.com

Table of Contents

Also by Madeline L. Stout:

Chapter Books:

Once Upon a Unicorn Series:

Once Upon a Unicorn - Book 1
Curse of the Seeker - Book 2
Journey to the Abyss - Book 3 (Fall 2017)

Picture Books:

The Moon Princess

For my mom.

Thank you for always supporting me in my dreams and endeavors, be it my imaginary herd of unicorns or just writing about them.

ONCE UPON A UNICORN

Presented by Fantasia Divinity

Chapter 1:

The Notebook

On the last day of fourth grade, I spent most of the day imagining how I was going to spend my summer. My head was full of stories that I had made up all day, and I couldn't wait to get home and act them out with my dolls. As an only child with two hardworking parents, entertaining myself was normal. And even though my dad, a teacher, was off most of the summer, he didn't like playing dolls with me.

Watching the clock anxiously, my hands inched to my bookbag, longing to pull out my old notebook. With only five minutes left before the bell, my will weakened. The purple notebook was worn on the edges and creased from lots of use. My mother gave it to me when I was four. It was usually kept at the bottom of a drawer in my bedroom, but today a strange feeling told me to take it out.

"What's that, Ora?" Savannah, the classroom bully, loomed up behind me.

"It's nothing," I said, trying to quickly shove it back into my backpack.

She yanked it from my hands and flipped through it. "Daydreaming about unicorns again?" she sneered. "I thought you finally grew up and realized those stupid things aren't real."

"I know they aren't real!" Would anyone let me forget the time I had an entire herd of imaginary unicorns? I had been convinced they were real. The notebook was where I used to draw pictures of them with their names so I could remember them all. When I was little, it never left my side.

"Grow up, Ora! You don't want to be a baby forever, do you?"

"I'm not a baby!" I'd been forced to accept the fact that unicorns weren't real, and as I did, my herd slowly vanished, leaving me alone once more.

The bell rang signaling the end of school and a wave of relief washed over me. I couldn't wait to get away from Savannah.

"Give me my notebook back, Savannah! It's time to go home."

"Sure, I'll give it back." With an evil smirk, she ripped out several pages and tore them in half.

"No!" I gasped.

My heart stopped as I watched the torn pages flutter to the floor.

Laughing, Savannah threw the rest of the notebook at me before sauntering out of the classroom.

I bent down to gather up the pieces. Tears stung my violet eyes. My world was shattered in that one moment.

Two ripped and crumpled pages in particular made me cry even more. My two favorites; Moonbeam and her daughter, Star. Moonbeam had been the queen, with a beautiful white coat, and a mane and tail of silvery purple.

They had stayed around long after all the other unicorns had left me.

Although I had accepted that I'd made them up long ago, it wasn't until seeing those torn pages that I truly felt they were gone. I straightened the pages as best I could and put them back into my bag. With a heavy heart, I began the long walk home.

Chapter 2:

Radona

Walking through the hayfield that separated the school from my house, I found a large roll of hay and climbed on top of it. Drying my tears, I pulled out my notebook. I missed my unicorns.

The wind whipped my red hair around my face and rustled the edges of the pages.

After several minutes, I heard the sound of hooves.

Looking up from my drawings, I saw a horse galloping towards me. The horse was a beautiful silvery-white color with a strange dark marking on its forehead. It almost looked like a crescent moon. The mare neighed at me and lowered her head. I was no stranger to horses; I started riding when I was very little. I smiled and pet her muzzle.

"Where did you come from, girl?" I asked, climbing off the hay.

The horse danced around me in little circles. I laughed at her antics. She lowered herself onto the ground and gestured with her head.

"Do you want me to ride you?"

She nodded.

I climbed onto her back and she stood. Holding tightly onto her mane, she took off at a fast gallop. Part of me wondered whether this was a good idea now that we were going so fast. Her speed did not bother me so much as the fact that she was taking me in a direction I was unfamiliar with.

She raced into the woods, dashing between the trees with ease. Up ahead, I could make out a large stone structure. It looked like a crumbling gateway from a long time ago.

The mare picked up speed and jumped in between the stone pillars. I closed my eyes and gave a small cry of surprise, gripping her mane even tighter. The breeze flew through my hair, and a mysterious tingling washed over my face.

When I opened my eyes again, it was like I had stepped into a dream.

We were in a field with grass far greener than any I had ever seen. Crystals littered the ground instead of rocks and trees glittered in the distance like beautiful jewels. Unicorns ran through the fields all around me and beautiful flowers bloomed behind them. I looked down at the mare who brought me here and gasped. Her mane and tail had turned a deep purple and a silver horn had grown in the middle of her crescent moon marking.

I had seen her before, but not for a very long time.

"Moonbeam?"

She turned her head to look back at me. "Hello, Ora."

My eyes widened, surprised.

"Welcome to the kingdom of Radona."

"Radona?" It was a name that held a vague familiarity to me. I thought back to when I was four and remembered it was the name I had given the kingdom of unicorns. But I had only made them up. Hadn't I?

"This is impossible. None of this is real," I said, although in my heart I wished for it to be true.

"I assure you, it is very real. Think back; who told you that unicorns aren't real?"

"My parents."

"Exactly. Most adults don't know we exist because other adults have told them so. And since they don't believe, they see what they want to see. In our case, just a regular horse."

"My mother once said she thought unicorns might have been real, but they were all gone from the world now," I said. "When I asked her what she thought might have happened to them, she said maybe they missed the ark when all the other animals were gathered up."

Moonbeam laughed. "Well, it is true that we left your world for some time after that unfortunate event, but we returned. There are many of us still in your world today. I was for a little while, as you'll recall."

"But I thought I made you all up." As I looked around the field, I realized that many of the unicorns around us were drawn in my notebook.

"No, Ora. We came to you. We saw how lonely you were and wanted to help you. Now, however, we need *your* help."

"For what?"

"Do you remember my daughter, Star?"

"Yes."

"She's in trouble. I need your help to save her."

"What's happened to her?"

"She's been kidnapped."

Chapter 3:

The Seeker

"Kidnapped? By who?" I asked.

"I'll explain the rest when we get to the palace."

Before I could say anything else, she bolted through the field, forcing me to grab onto her mane once more.

We galloped for several minutes until at last I saw a large castle appear in the distance. It had two large spires on the sides, one shaped like a crescent moon, and another with curving halls off the sides making it look like the sun. When we reached its gates, two unicorn guards opened them for us to pass through.

"Welcome back, Your Majesty," one of the guards said with a deep bow.

"Thank you. Where is my little sister?" Moonbeam replied.

"In the courtyard. She is eagerly awaiting your return."

Moonbeam nodded and passed through the gates and into the castle.

We entered a stone courtyard where a young woman ran up to us. Her hair was a beautiful blend of red and gold, her eyes like the sun.

"Moonbeam! Thank goodness you're back! I've been so worried that something would happen to you!"

"I'm fine, sister."

"Wait, that's your sister? But she's human!" I said in surprise.

"Human? I may be many things, my dear Ora, but human is certainly not one of them," the young woman replied.

"How do you know my name?"

"Do you not remember me at all? Perhaps this will help." She held out her arms and leaned her head back.

That was when I noticed it. On her forehead, a horn like a unicorn's sat in the middle of a sun marking. The tip of the horn began to glow and surround her in a bright light. I shielded my eyes until it died down.

When I looked again, the woman was gone. In her place, stood another unicorn. One I recognized.

"Sunspear?"

"See? You do remember me!" Sunspear cried happily.

Moonbeam lowered herself to the floor and I climbed off her back.

"But you were a human just a moment ago."

"Unicorns possess magic, and with it we can change our forms. Sometimes it's easier to do things when you have hands," Moonbeam said with a smile.

"Yeah, I guess you're right."

"I have an errand to run. I'll be back in a moment," Moonbeam said before turning.

"All right." I watched her go.

A second later, a guard came in needing to speak with Sunspear. Left alone, I decided to follow Moonbeam, my curiosity urging me forward.

Moonbeam quickly walked down the crystal corridors as I lagged a safe distance behind. She came to a large set of double doors. Using the magic from her horn, she threw the doors open and entered a dark room.

I hurried to catch the door before it closed behind her, then quietly slipped in. It was a circular room with a large blue flame floating in the center. The flame cast very little light.

"Seeker, my daughter has been taken, and my trust betrayed," Moonbeam spoke to the floating blue flame. "You once told me that if any trouble should arise, I would need the one who can see. I would need Ora. I have brought her to Rodona as you suggested."

"Good," the Seeker said slowly.

"What else should I do? Where has he taken her?"

"She is in the abandoned fortress," the Seeker said.

"Then I will bring her back." Moonbeam turned for the door.

"There is more."

Moonbeam stopped and looked back to the Seeker.

"You cannot retrieve her on your own," the Seeker continued. "You must take the girl. She is the key."

"Very well."

My eyes widened.

The key? The key to what? I snuck back out of the room and hurried to the courtyard where Moonbeam had originally taken me. I returned right before Sunspear. A moment later, Moonbeam joined us again as well.

"Any news on the princess?" Sunspear asked, turning to Moonbeam.

Moonbeam shook her head.

"What happened to her? Who took her?" I asked, looking at Moonbeam.

"Zentis, one of my servants."

"Why would he do that?"

"I wish I knew. Zentis was always a good boy. A little quiet maybe, but a hard worker. Loyal. Or so I thought," Moonbeam answered sadly.

"A guard spoke with me while you were gone. We believe that he has taken her to an abandoned underground fortress," Sunspear said.

"Yes, that is what the Seeker said as well."

"Why would he take her there?" I asked them.

"It's heavily guarded. The fortress used to belong to the unicorns, long ago, but we were driven out by dragons," Moonbeam answered. "The fortress is located inside a mountain. There are several cave entrances, but many have collapsed now."

"If you know who took her, and where she is, then what do you need me for?"

"The Seeker said you were the key to returning Star."

"The Seeker? Who is that?" I knew from what I had just witnessed that it was a strange blue flame, but I had no idea what it actually was and how it knew the location of the princess.

"An oracle of sorts. You're special Ora, and we need someone special if there is any hope of getting my daughter back."

"I'm not special, not like you. The two of you have magic, I don't have anything."

"You do, you just don't see it yet."

Chapter 4:

The Dragon

Sunspear stayed behind at the castle, while Moonbeam and I went after Princess Star. We rode through the forest in silence. My thoughts were full of everything that Sunspear and

Moonbeam had said. I still didn't know how I could possibly help, but I certainly wanted to try.

When we reached the end of the woods, Moonbeam stopped. Ahead of us was a tall mountain, capped in snow.

"The fortress is in there."

"How do we get inside? Do you know where the entrance is?"

"Yes. Do you see that space between the two mountain peaks? There is a cave there that should lead us right to the heart of the mountain."

The space she was talking about was quite high up the mountain.

"But how are we going to get up there?" I didn't like the idea of having to climb that far.

"We fly, of course!" she said with a laugh.

"We… wait, what?" My eyes widened as the tip of her horn started to glow. Her fur grew hot beneath my legs. Light formed on her sides and took shape. Beautiful shimmery wings made of feathers and light fluttered on either side of me.

"Wow!" I gasped as I ran my hand over one of them. "I wish I could do that!"

"Maybe one day, you can. Now hold on tight, Ora!"

I held onto her mane as she flapped her large gossamer wings. She leapt into the air and we left the ground far behind.

Wind roared around us as we lifted higher and higher. I closed my eyes, loving the feel of it running its invisible fingers through my long hair.

When we landed, I dismounted and looked around. It was like we were in some kind of crater set in between the two mountain peaks. High walls of rock surrounded us on all sides. Ahead of us, there was a large cave opening.

Filled with a strange sense of dread, I stumbled back a few steps. Rocks hung down forming sharp points over the entrance. They looked like teeth.

"That's the only way in?" I asked, my voice shaking.

Moonbeam nodded. "Be on your guard, Ora. This is dragon territory now."

"I like dragons…"

"That may be, but they probably won't like you. Especially while you are with me."

"Why is that?" Curiosity overpowered my fear and I approached the opening cautiously, looking for a dragon.

"Unicorns and dragons don't get along. Dragons are territorial and jealous creatures by nature. They have no magic of their own and envy ours. They fear we will use it to take away their treasure."

"And won't you?"

I jumped at the sound of a strange voice behind me. I turned and saw a large dragon perched on a rock.

The dragon's eyes glowed gold, almost like the gold coins I had always read about them collecting. Her scales were green and glittered in the sun.

"I have no interest in your treasure, dragon." Moonbeam said, turning to face it.

"Then why are you here? Unicorns are not welcome, as I am sure you know, Queen Moonbeam."

"It seems you have me at a bit of a disadvantage. You know my name, but I do not know yours."

"My name is Emeraldis. Now you and your human friend need to leave here."

"Please, Emeraldis." I rushed forward in front of Moonbeam. "We are not here to bother you. We are just looking for someone."

"Whoever it is, you will not find them here."

"We think they are inside the mountain. Her daughter…"

"Ora, no!" Moonbeam said, cutting me off. She trotted in front of me and used her magic to turn into her humanoid form. Like her unicorn form, her hair was a sparkling purple and her skin a shimmering white. She wore a long, slimming white dress with moon accents and an elegant crown. "We can't trust her."

"Why? Because she's a dragon? We need her help." I looked back up at the dragon. "Her daughter has been taken, and we believe that whoever did it has her in this mountain. Can you help us find her?"

"Why should I help you?" Emeraldis asked, regarding me closely.

"I don't know why there is such animosity between the dragons and the unicorns, but it doesn't matter. Her daughter is in trouble. You should want to help because it is the right thing to do." I turned to look at Moonbeam. Her arms were crossed and she had an expression that clearly indicated she believed I was wasting my time. Maybe I was.

"And if that's not enough reason," I paused, looking around, "maybe we can work out some kind of deal?"

Emeraldis' eyes narrowed. "What did you have in mind?"

"Uhm… jewels! Dragons like treasure, so we'll give you jewels if you help us." I looked to Moonbeam who nodded her consent.

Emeraldis scoffed. "Do you truly think that all dragons are exactly alike? My desires are not so simple as that."

"All right, then what is it that you want?"

Emeraldis thought a moment before answering. "Magic," she whispered.

"Magic? Dragons can't perform magic," Moonbeam said next to me.

"I'm well aware. She asked what I desired, and that is it."

"And if you had magic, what would you do with it?" I asked, stopping Moonbeam before she could say anything else.

"I would become human."

Chapter 5:

More Precious than Gold

"Human?" Moonbeam asked skeptically.

"Yes. I want to be able to take on a human form when I wish like you unicorns do."

I turned to Moonbeam. "Can you do that?"

"I suppose there is a way." Using her magic, she made an emerald necklace appear in her hand. Her horn sent out a blast of purple magical energy that pulsed and surrounded it. When the light subsided, she held it out to Emeraldis. "This necklace is now enchanted with unicorn magic. When you wear it, you will have the power to change your form at will, from dragon to human, and back again."

Emeraldis flew down from her rocky perch and landed in front of Moonbeam.

"You are certain it will work?"

"Yes."

I took the necklace from Moonbeam's hand and fastened it around Emeraldis' large neck.

"Go on, try it," I said excitedly.

"How? I've never used magic before."

"Me either, but I remember reading once that magic is all in the heart and mind. If you can see it in your mind and believe it in your heart, then you can do anything."

"She's right. If you want to be a human girl, then just visualize yourself as human."

Emeraldis closed her large reptilian eyes. Green and gold energy swirled around her large form, the ball of light getting smaller and smaller until it was just a little larger than me.

Inside the light, I saw the shape of a young woman form. The light faded and Emeraldis opened her eyes.

"Did it work?" She looked at her hands and gasped. She touched her face and felt the long hair cascading around her. Her eyes were the same dazzling gold but now she had the hair to match. She wore a dress of brilliant emerald that matched the color of her former scales. "I'm human!"

"And you will remain so as long as you wear that necklace," Moonbeam said, pointing to the emerald pendant around her neck.

Emeraldis touched the necklace and smiled. "Thank you. Maybe I was wrong about you, after all."

"Will you help us find the princess now?" I asked.

"Of course. I will tell you what I can. You were right about them being here. I saw three figures enter the caverns, all in cloaks, all in human form. The tallest carried a smaller one in his arms."

"You didn't stop them?" Moonbeam asked with a hint of anger.

"I was going to, but I got a bad feeling from one of them. I couldn't see much, but I did see her eyes. They were like ice. I could sense great power in her, but there was something off about it. I decided that whoever she was, she was someone that I didn't want to mess with."

I turned to look at Moonbeam. "Do you know who that could have been?"

"It might have been Azarinth, Zentis' older sister. She's a powerful sorceress at the court. She has eyes like you described. She's always been cold and distant. I admit that I don't know much about her."

"I guess she decided to help her brother then," I said.

"Or it was her idea. I'd actually believe that far more than him."

"We better get going if we are going to catch up to them." I turned back to Emeraldis. "Thank you for your help."

"Good luck, I hope you find the princess." She waved to us as we turned and entered the cave.

Chapter 6:

The Ice Sorceress

The cave was dark and damp, and a cold wind echoed throughout. The path was narrow, forcing Moonbeam to maintain her human shape.

We walked in silence for several minutes until a strange scratching sound up ahead caught my attention. "What was that?"

"Hello, Your Majesty. We've been expecting you." A woman appeared before us. From her tail and horn, I guessed she was a unicorn as well. She was hauntingly beautiful; light violet skin and hair that was a mix of deep purple and burgundy. Her eyes were icy blue, just as Emeraldis had described.

"Give me back my daughter, Azarinth!"

"I don't have her," she said, shrugging.

"Maybe not, but you know where she is."

"And if I do?" Azarinth said with a playful smile.

"Just tell us where she is. We don't want to fight you," I said.

"Hm... No. I'm bored now..." Azarinth raised one of her hands and shot an icy blast towards us.

Moonbeam jumped in front of me and conjured a magic barrier to block the attack.

"That little shield won't protect you for long!" Azarinth laughed and raised her hand to her mouth, blowing a thousand small ice crystals against the barrier, peppering it with cracks. The cracks grew until the whole thing shattered.

"Ora, stay behind me!"

"But I want to help!"

She didn't hear me as she dodged another attack and launched her own counter attack.

I was helpless. I wanted to do something, anything, to help. Looking around the cave, I had an idea. The unicorns were too absorbed in their fight to pay attention to what I was doing.

I followed a small path leading upwards as far as I could before climbing up a large boulder. I climbed until I was almost touching the cave ceiling. The rocks next to me looked unsteady, as if a small push would send them all crashing down. I waited until Azarinth was directly under the rocks, then I shoved them as hard as I could.

The rocks tumbled to the ground in a great clatter of noise, and Azarinth cried out from below. But more rocks fell than I was expecting. The stones beneath my hands gave way and I slipped from my perch.

I screamed as I joined the falling rocks on their journey to the ground. Closing my eyes, I braced myself against the coming impact. I shouted in surprise when instead of landing on the hard ground, someone caught me. Moonbeam smiled down at me.

"It's okay, I've got you. That was a brilliant plan you had!"

"Did it work?" I asked as she set me back on the ground.

"It did; knocked her out cold, so to speak," she said with a giggle. "That should give us plenty of time to reach the fortress and find Star."

I smiled.

We continued our trek through the cave until we reached a large open cavern. My eyes widened as I looked around. A massive stone fortress was built into the walls of the cave and reached up all the way to the top of the mountain.

"Your daughter is in there?"

"Yes, somewhere."

"How are we going to find her? This place is huge!"

"We'll find a way, we just have to believe."

I nodded and the two of us walked up to the large stone doors.

Chapter 7:

Zentis

The doors opened onto what looked like a large throne room. Magic flames danced along the walls casting a dim light. There were two doors at the back of the room. I was about to ask which one we should take when a dark shadow appeared in front of us.

A black unicorn with a mane and tail of silver came out of the shadow.

"Leave this place now."

"Where is my daughter, Zentis?"

"She is safe with me, I assure you."

"How safe can she be? You kidnapped her!" Moonbeam shouted.

"I have no intention of harming her."

"If you don't want to hurt Princess Star, then just release her," I said.

"I'm afraid I can't do that." Zentis charged and Moonbeam quickly turned back into her unicorn form.

She met him head on and their horns clashed together sending off sparks of magic.

Oh no! I have to do something!

Zentis looked beyond the point of negotiating now, and there weren't any rocks I could use like before. What could I do?

Think Ora, think!

The fight wore on, but still I could think of nothing that would help.

"This ends now!" Zentis yelled. He looked like he was going to charge her again, and Moonbeam prepared to block, but right before the strike, he changed form.

Something drove me forward and I pushed Moonbeam out of the way.

A small blade materialized in his hand.

I screamed as a sharp pain pierced my arm. Moonbeam cried out and I fell to the floor, holding my arm.

"You'll pay for hurting her!" She unleashed a large blast of light that sent Zentis flying across the room, where he slammed hard against the wall.

Moonbeam rushed to my side. She lowered her head and touched the tip of her horn to my injured arm. A strange warmth filled me and the pain eased.

"You'll be all right now."

"Thank you." I stood up, rubbing my sore arm, and looked to the unicorn on the floor. "I guess now we can search for your daughter."

Before Moonbeam could answer, a scream resounded behind us.

"No! Zentis! What have you done to him?"

I turned and saw a young girl.

Moonbeam gasped. "Star?"

Chapter 8:

A Blind Rage

"*That's* Star?"

The girl in front of me certainly didn't look like she had been kidnapped. In fact, she looked angry that we were there. Her mystic pink eyes filled with tears as she slowly approached Zentis.

She knelt down and brushed the hair away from his face before she turned back around to us.

"What did you do?" She raged, her eyes turning a deep red.

"Star, it's me, your mother. I came to get you back."

"I don't want to go back! Not with you!" Star unleashed a beam of red, hot magic towards Moonbeam, forcing her to jump out of the way.

"Why doesn't she look happy to see you?" I yelled, as I crouched behind a rock to hide from her attacks.

"I don't know. Maybe they cast some sort of spell on her?"

"Then how do we break it?"

"I'm not sure."

"We better figure it out, she's pretty angry!"

Moonbeam galloped towards her daughter, blocking each of her attacks with her horn.

There's something not right here... My eyes darted from Star's tear-stained face to Zentis' unconscious form on the floor. *Hm...*

It didn't make sense to me that Star would be this upset over a kidnapper.

Unless... I jumped out from behind my hiding spot and ran to Zentis.

There was a small cut on his forehead.

"The only reason she would be this upset, is if she wasn't really kidnapped at all," I murmured to myself.

"I need to wake him up, to show Star that he is okay. Then they will stop fighting."

But how? I need magic... if only I could heal him like Moonbeam healed me.

"I wonder…" It was a long shot, but a small voice inside told me that I should try.

I held my hands out over his head and closed my eyes. In my mind, I focused on what I wanted. I saw myself healing him. I imagined his wound closing.

My hands grew warm. I looked down and saw them glow with a brilliant golden light. Zentis' wound healed and his eyes fluttered opened.

"I did it!"

"What happened?" Zentis asked as he sat up groggily.

"Did you kidnap Star, or did she go with you willingly?" I asked him quickly.

He looked at me before he reluctantly spoke. "No, I didn't. I love her, but she's a princess... so we ran."

"We have to stop them. Fighting isn't going to accomplish anything."

Chapter 9:

Love Conquers All

Zentis stood on shaky legs and approached the two dueling unicorns.

"Star! Stop!" He yelled.

Star turned. The red in her eyes faded when she saw him.

"Zentis, you're all right!" She ran up to him and flung her arms around his neck.

"It's okay Star, I'm fine," he said stroking her purple and pink hair.

"What is going on here?" Moonbeam demanded.

"They're in love. He didn't kidnap her, they ran away so that they could be together." I moved to stand beside Moonbeam.

"What?" Her eyes widened as she looked toward her daughter. "But why didn't she tell me?"

"I was afraid," Star said, turning to face her mother. "I know the laws, but I don't want to marry someone of noble birth, and I know it is your job to uphold those laws. So instead of doing something that might cause conflict for you, we left."

"On top of that, the stress of her royal duties has really been taking a toll on her. She's been ill; overcome with these episodes of rage followed by exhaustion. I wanted to get her away from all of that, no matter the cost." Zentis added.

"And you didn't think that running away would cause me conflict?" Moonbeam stared at Star. "I have been worried sick about you, my dear!"

"I'm sorry, Mother. I didn't want to hurt you." Star hung her head in shame.

"It's all right, my darling. Just please, come home with me."

Star turned to look at Zentis. "What about him? As he said, he really was just trying to help. My magic has been crazy lately, playing with my emotions."

"While I don't approve of his method of helping, I realize his heart was in the right place. He can come as well." Moonbeam smiled and hugged her daughter. "We will do what we have to in order to treat your ailment."

"Thank you, Mother."

"You can always come and talk with me when something is bothering you. I may be queen, but I am also your mother. I love you very much, never forget that."

Chapter 10:

Home Again

We flew back to the palace and everyone cheered when they saw their princess return.

Sunspear ran out of the palace to greet us and drew her niece into a tight hug. "I'm so glad you're back, Star."

"Me too." Star smiled.

Moonbeam explained to everyone what happened. Zentis and his sister were cleared of all charges.

Star walked up to me while everyone else was busy planning a celebration.

"I just wanted to thank you for what you did," she said.

"I didn't really do anything. I don't even know why your mother wanted me to go along."

"But you did a lot! Zentis told me how you healed him. Without you there, things could have gone very differently."

"I don't even know how I did it."

"It doesn't matter, what's important is that you did. I'm sure we will understand the rest in time."

"Are you ready to go back to your own world now, Ora?" Moonbeam asked as she approached us.

"I wish I could stay here with all of you, but… yeah, I think I want to go back and see my own mother now."

Moonbeam smiled. "All right, let's go, but don't despair, we will see you again soon. I will come and get you when it is time for Star's wedding."

***

When I got home that night, it turned out that very little time had passed in my world. What felt like a day in Radona, was really only an hour.

I ran inside and threw my arms around my own mother. "I love you, Mommy!"

"I love you too, Ora. What's gotten into you?" my mother said, hugging me back.

"I just missed you, that's all."

"You saw me this morning." She looked down at me skeptically.

"A lot has happened since then!"

"Like what?" She laughed.

"Like unicorns…"

"Unicorns?" The skepticism was back.

"How about tonight instead of you reading me a bedtime story, I'll tell you one."

"All right." My mother ruffled my hair with a smile.

"Good!" I grinned. "I think you're going to really like it." Together, the two of us sat down and I explained everything that had happened.

And I was right. She did like my story.

Preview:

Once Upon a Unicorn vol. 2: Curse of the Seeker

Chapter 1

Everything was dark. My eyes were open, unseeing, as they stared into a black abyss. Slowly, the darkness moved. Shadows formed and took shape to create an image. I was standing in a strange room. I knew this room; I had seen it before. It was the Chamber of Knowledge inside Queen Moonbeam's castle. The blue flame known as the Seeker appeared before me, taking its normal position in the center. The flame pulsed and grew.

"The time has come," the Seeker's voice echoed off the stone walls of the room. It was loud, commanding. "The magic keeping me sealed is weakening." The flame grew ever brighter, overtaking the room. "I can be free."

A pulse went out from the flame so strong that it knocked me back. Pain seared through my chest as the air left my lungs. My head collided with the stone wall behind me sending shockwaves of pain throughout my being. My eyes closed and I knew only darkness once more.

***

I woke with a jolt, heart racing in my chest. My eyes quickly scanned the room and I breathed a sigh of relief to see I was still in my bedroom. I took a few deep, shuddery breaths and willed my heart to calm down. There was a strange ache in my head, a vague reference to the bizarre dream I just had.

What was that? Of everything that I went through in Radona, why would I dream about the Seeker?

The sun shone brightly through my window, acting as a soothing balm.

It was just a dream. It meant nothing.

I got up and began my day.

***

"Ora, have you gotten all the blackberries yet?" my mom called from the house.

I was knee deep in a blackberry bush, reaching for the plump ones at the center.

"Coming, Mommy!" I picked the last berry and climbed out of the tangled branches. I ran back to the house and gave my mom the basket.

Out of the corner of my eye, something moved.

I turned and saw a beautiful Appaloosa run behind a large oak in our backyard. The sun gleamed on the horse and the light caught something on her head.

That almost looks like ... a horn!

My breath caught. Excitement filled me as I turned back to my mother.

"Mommy, can I go out and play for a little while?"

"Yeah, just be back by dark," she replied with a smile.

"OK! Thanks!" I rushed out the door and looked for the horse.

Her head peered out from behind a tree in the wooded area that surrounded our house.

"There you are!" I went to her and ran my hands along her soft neck. "Is it time for the wedding?" I asked.

The horse nodded. I quickly mounted her using a tall stump and held on tight.

"I'm ready."

She took off along the same path Moonbeam had taken me the last time. My heart raced as we jumped through the portal, a smile plastered on my face.

I took a deep breath, trying to contain my excitement. Once again, I was surrounded by unicorns.

About the Author

Madeline L. Stout started writing when she was a little girl and completed her first full-length novel at the age of 15. Mostly, she loves creating fantasy worlds filled with beautiful creatures and strong heroines. When her husband insists she takes a break from writing, she enjoys reading and gaming. Madeline is the founder and editor-in-chief of *Fantasia Divinity.* She is the author of *The Moon Princess* and the children's series, *Once Upon a Unicorn.*

CPSIA information can be obtained
at www.ICGtesting.com
Printed in the USA
LVHW111300260320
651282LV00001B/185